Postman Pat's
Sore Tooth
Story by **John Cunliffe**
Pictures by **Joan Hickson**

From the original Television designs by **Ivor Wood**

André Deutsch/Hippo Books

Published in hardback in 1989 by André Deutsch Limited
105-106 Great Russell Street, London WC1B 3LJ
and in paperback by Hippo Books,
Scholastic Publications Limited
10 Earlham Street, London WC2 9RX
Second impression 1990

ISBN 0 233 98395 3 (hardback)
ISBN 0 590 76184 6 (paperback)

Made and printed in Belgium by Proost

Pat was eating his cornflakes.

"Ooooh!" he said.

And,

"Ouch!" he said.

Jess came to see what was wrong.

"It's all right," said Pat. "It's only a tooth. I'll eat on the other side. It'll soon be better. Do cats ever get toothache?"

Jess had nothing to say about that. He was busy having his morning wash.

Pat finished his cornflakes, and his
toast-and-marmalade, and his coffee.
Jess finished his milk. Then it was time
to be on their way. Pat's tooth had
stopped aching. It was a sunny
morning. Pat sang a cheerful song as
he drove along the winding Greendale
roads. He had forgotten his sore tooth.

At the village post-office, Mrs. Goggins had a lot of letters for Pat.

"Would you like a toffee," she said.

"Oooh, thanks," said Pat.

He never could say, "No " to a toffee. But he had just begun to chew it, when he shouted, "Owwwwww!" dropped his letters all over the floor, did a little dance, and pulled the toffee out of his mouth. A piece of tooth came with it.

"Oh, dear," said Mrs. Goggins.

"Ooooh! Ow! Ouch!" said Pat.

Mrs. Goggins ran to the bathroom,
and came back with a little green
bottle and a piece of cotton-wool.

"Toothache tincture," she said. "My mum always said this was best for toothache. Now, Pat, can you just keep still, and open your mouth wide, and I'll dab a bit of this on your tooth. Which one is it? Do keep still, it's going on your tongue. There, I've got a good dab at it."

Pat knew she had.

"Oooooh! Ow-wow!" he yelled.

His tooth was hurting more than ever with Mrs. Goggins' dabbing. She dripped more of the stuff from the bottle on to a blob of cotton-wool. "Now hold that gently on your tooth, and it'll soon feel better," she said.

Pat sat down in Mrs. Goggins' armchair, nursing his tooth. Mrs. Goggins gathered up all his letters, and sorted them out again.

"There's one here for Dr. Gilbertson," she said. "You'd best have a word with her about your tooth. I expect she'll send you off to the dentist in Pencaster."

"Oh, dear," said Pat. He didn't like going to the dentist's.

After a time, Pat's tooth felt a little better, and he set out with his letters.

Doctor Gilbertson was out, so Pat popped her letters through the door.

At the village school, Pat saw a chart on the wall about teeth, and how to take care of them.

"Now you make sure you brush your teeth," he said to Katy and Tom, talking with the side of his mouth that wasn't sore.

"Why are you talking funny?" said Katy.

"Am I?" said Pat. "Must rush. Lots of post. Bye!"

Back in his van, he wrote a note on the back of his hand.

"Get brush," it said.

Pat called on Granny Dryden with her
new catalogue.

"Have you got toothache?" she said.

"I have," said Pat. "How did you
guess?"

"I can tell," she said. "You're
talking funny, and you're looking
glum. I've got just the thing for it."

She brought an old tin from the kitchen. It had such a smell when she opened it! She gave Pat a hard little round thing.

"Suck that," she said. "You'll soon feel better."

"What is it?" said Pat.

"Nutmeg," said Granny Dryden. "My old dad always used it for toothache. It never failed."

"I'll give it a try," said Pat.

Pat was on his way.

His tooth felt much better.

Then he called on Ted.

Ted gave Pat a mug of coffee. It was very hot; straight from Ted's stove. And that started the tooth off again.

"We'll tie some string on it," said Ted, "and I'll give it a good pull. We'll have it out in no time."

"No thanks," said Pat, and he hurried away before Ted could find his string.

Pat called on Miss Hubbard. His tooth was really bad again. His face was all screwed up with the pain.

"You silly man," said Miss Hubbard. "You must go to the dentist at once."

"Oh dear," said Pat. "I don't like the dentist's."

But Miss Hubbard was having none of that. She sat Pat in a chair, and wouldn't let him get up.

"Won't be a minute," said Miss
Hubbard. "You just sit here, quietly."
Pat heard the tinkle of the telephone.
"It's all arranged," said Miss
Hubbard. "Not a thing to worry
about."

Ten minutes later, Pat was on his way
to Pencaster in Alf's Landrover, with
Miss Hubbard in the back with Jess on
her knee.

At the dentist's, Miss Hubbard
whisked Pat past the queue, saying,
"Excuse me! Urgent case!"

And Pat was in the dentist's chair
before he had time to feel frightened.

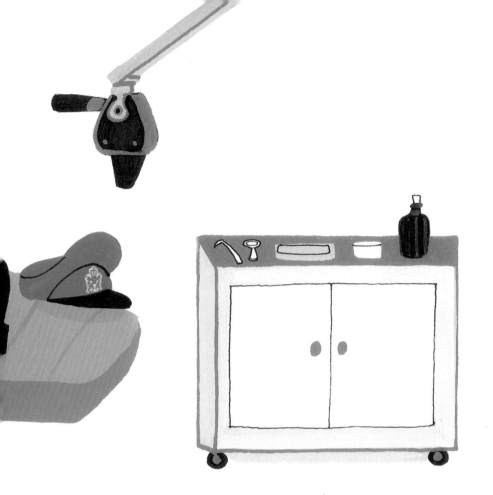

"Now, could we just have a look,"
said a gentle voice. "Nothing to worry
about. Just open your mouth as widely
as you can."

"What a nice dentist," thought Pat.

When Pat came out of the dentist's room, he was smiling again.

"How did you get on?" said Miss Hubbard.

"Great!" said Pat. "She's a lovely dentist, and it didn't hurt a bit."

"How's the tooth?" said Miss Hubbard.

"Fine!" said Pat. "It doesn't hurt at all now. She's put a filling in it, and I'm coming back for a check-up next week."

"Good," said Miss Hubbard.

"And I've got a brush and a free tube of toothpaste," said Pat, rubbing the note off his hand.

And just as they were leaving the dentist's, who should they meet coming in but Mrs. Pottage with Katy and Tom!

"Hello," said Pat. "Fancy meeting you. Do you come here often?"

"Of course we do," said Katy, "don't you?"

"Well . . . I'm going to," said Pat.

And he did.

The dentist gave him a card so that he wouldn't forget to have his check-ups, and he didn't miss a single time.

Pat never had toothache again. And if he ever met anyone with toothache, he would say,

"Get yourself off to the dentist. She's great!"